Published by
Delacorte Press
Bantam Doubleday Dell Publishing Group, Inc.
666 Fifth Avenue
New York, New York 10103
This edition was originally published in Great Britain in 1988 by Hodder and
Stoughton Children's Books, a division of Hodder and Stoughton Ltd.
Text and illustrations
Copyright © Nick Butterworth and Mick Inkpen 1988
The trademark Delacorte Press® is registered in the
U.S. Patent and Trademark Office.

Library of Congress Cataloging-in-Publication Data

Butterworth, Nick.
Field Day / Nick Butterworth and Mick Inkpen.
p.   cm.
Summary: Parents and children participate in the Field Day races.
ISBN 0-385-30328-9 — ISBN 0-385-30329-7 (lib. bdg.)
[1. Racing — Fiction.]   I. Inkpen, Mick.   II. Title
PZ7.B98225Fi   1991
[E] — dc20   90-49467   CIP   AC

Manufactured in U.S.A.

July 1991

10   9   8   7   6   5   4   3   2   1

FIELD DAY

Nick Butterworth and Mick Inkpen

Delacorte Press   New York

Hooray! Today is Field Day.
Sam is training hard. He's eaten all his breakfast
and now he's doing his exercises.
Tracy is still in bed. She says she's saving her
energy for later.

"Good luck," says Dad as he goes off to work.
Mom is listening for the weather forecast.
"... *and later, showers threatening the area.*"

It's a lovely afternoon. It looks like the
weatherman was wrong.
Lots of moms and dads have come to watch.
"Welcome to our Field Day, everybody," says
Mrs. Jefferson. But the bullhorn isn't working
properly and nobody can hear.
She gives it a shake and tries again. Still it
won't work.
Mr. Bryant, the handyman, comes to help.
He switches it on.

The first race is for the kindergarteners.
It's a bean bag race.
"Stand back behind the line," says Ms. Foster.
"Ready. Set. Go."
They're off.
Jeffrey's bean bag has fallen off his head.
Jenny's is slipping off too.
Matthew's won't come off. He's holding it on.

The next race is the wheelbarrow race.
"Now, pushers, don't push too hard," says Ms. Foster.
"We don't want any broken wheels."
David and Jamie are making a lot of noise.
"We're being a space buggy,"
says Jamie.
"Spacemen need to be extra careful,"
says Ms. Foster
Away they go!
Everybody shouts and cheers.
It's going to be close. . . .
At the finish the space buggy
is just beaten by a
wheelbarrow.

Karen has to use crutches to help her
get around. She's going to run in the fifty-meter dash.
Ms. Foster says that Karen can start a little in
front if she likes. But Karen doesn't want to.
They're off and running.
Look at Karen go! She's going to come in third.
Go, Karen!
There's a great big cheer
as she crosses the finish line.
After the race everyone
wants to try
Karen's crutches.

Sam and his friend Richard are revving up at the
starting line like two racing cars. Brrrmmm!
They're in the egg and spoon race.
Ms. Foster says, "Go!" and they're off.
The girls are going very carefully, especially Tania.
She isn't going to be first. But she isn't going to
drop her egg.

Sam is doing well. Very well. He's going to win!
"Oh, no!" Richard has dropped his egg and it's broken!
It's run all over his shoe.
One of the teachers wipes it off.
"Your mom was supposed to
give you a hard-boiled
egg," she says.

Oh, dear. Where have those clouds come from?
It looks like the weatherman was right after all.
Let's hope it's just a passing shower.
On go the coats. Up go the umbrellas.
Tracy's mom didn't bring an umbrella.
But she did bring a thermos.
"Would you like some coffee, Ms. Foster?"
"Thank you," says Ms. Foster. "It's brightening up
a bit now."

Good. The rain has stopped. The sun comes out and
the umbrellas start to steam.
Tracy is in the next race. It's the obstacle race.
"Run backward to the hoops," says Ms. Foster, "then
through the hoops, under the sheet, into the sacks,
and hop to the finish. Are you ready? Go!"

Tracy's off to a good start.
Oh, dear. Joanne's hoop is stuck.
Tracy's the first one under the sheet.
Matthew's found a hole in it.
Now what's happening?
There's a lot of wriggling and giggling under the sheet.
But no one's coming out.
"I think we'd better help them out," says Ms. Foster.
No one wins. But it was good fun.

The last race of the afternoon is the dad's race.

"My dad's a great runner," says Henry.

"So is mine," says Paul.

The dads are all laughing as they wait for the start.

"Go!"

They're off. Oops! Henry's dad has lost a sandal.

Nicola's dad wins. Henry's dad is last.

"Don't cry, Henry," says Ms. Foster.

But Henry says he's just got
something in his eye.

And now it's time to go home.
"Well done, everybody," says Mrs. Jefferson, and she
thanks everyone for coming. But no one can hear.
Mr. Bryant has put the bullhorn away.

"Did you see me win, Mom?" says Sam.
"I certainly did," says Mom.
"Look, there's Dad!" shouts Tracy. "Come on, Sam.
I'll race you to the gate!"